ALADDIN

An imprint of Simon & Schuster Children's Publishing Division

1230 Avenue of the Americas, New York, New York 10020

This Aladdin hardcover edition September 2016

For information about special discounts for bulk purchases, please contact Simon & Schuster Special Sales at 1-866-506-1949 or business@simonandschuster.com.

The Simon & Schuster Speakers Bureau can bring authors to your live event. For more information or to book an event contact the Simon & Schuster Speakers Bureau at 1-866-248-3049 or visit our website at www.simonspeakers.com.

Cover designed by Gail Ghezzi and Steve Scott

Interior designed by Jennifer Blanc and Steve Scott

The illustrations for this book were rendered digitally.

The text of this book was set in Vendome.

Manufactured in China 0716 SCP

2 4 6 8 10 9 7 5 3 1

Library of Congress Control Number 2015946384

ISBN 978-1-4814-6612-7 (POB)

ISBN 978-0-689-83468-4 (hc)

To my mother, for all the bedtime stories —R. P. E.

For my wife, Kim —D. C.

igh in the mountains, where the clouds lie on the ground like great cotton balls, is the Christmas town of Noel.

N O E L

Noel is surrounded by tall, white city walls
that sparkle in the sun and city gates of pure silver,
striped red like candy sticks. In the center of the
town is a square where a tall Christmas tree is
decorated all year long. But even more important
than the tree is the great brass Christmas torch next
to it. For it is here, on Christmas Eve, that the
Keeper of the Flame comes to light the torch,
bringing the brightness and warmth of
Christmas to the entire world.

In the hills outside the town of Noel lived a small boy named Alexander. Every Christmas Eve, Alexander and his mother walked many miles to the town square to see the lighting of the flame. But the last few years it had been too difficult for his mother to make the long walk, and Alexander had to go alone.

Only a week before Christmas, Alexander ran into their small cottage. "Have you heard, Mother? This year the Keeper of the Flame will choose someone new to light the torch."

"Who will he choose?"

"Whoever gives the truest gift of Christmas." Then Alexander frowned. "I wish that I had something special to give," he said. "I would like to light the Christmas torch."

His mother put her arms around her son. "You are a good boy. I could not be more proud of you if you were the Keeper of the Flame himself."

Early in the morning of Christmas Eve, Alexander prepared for his trip to the town square. His mother put a loaf of bread, a chunk of cheese, and a jar of hot cider in his pack. Then she bundled him up in an extra cloak, as it was snowing outside.

"Remember, Alexander, after the lighting of the flame it will be late. You must spend the night at the town church. I will expect you back tomorrow afternoon."

Alexander kissed his mother good-bye, then started on the long walk to Noel.

After walking most of the day, Alexander could hear the bells of Noel ringing in the distance, calling the people to the square. Soon they would shut the city's great gate, and no one would be allowed inside during the lighting of the flame. Alexander walked faster.

As he neared the city gate, he noticed a small bundle of cloth in the snow.

"Someone has dropped their cloak," Alexander said. Then he saw that it was not just a cloak, but an old man. Alexander knelt next to the man. He took off his gloves and rubbed the man's face with his warm hands. The man's eyes slowly opened. Alexander took the hot cider from his pack. "Here," Alexander said. "Drink this. It will warm you."

The man looked at Alexander. "Who are you? An angel?"

"I am Alexander."

The man smiled. "Thank you, Alexander."

"I'm too small to lift you. I will get help in the city," Alexander said. He put his extra cloak around the old man.

Alexander ran through the city gates to find someone to help him. But no one would leave the square.

"The gates will soon close," they all said. "We would miss the lighting."

Then the large gates did begin to close. Alexander looked at the beautiful tall Christmas tree and the great torch in the square, then back at the gate. With all his heart he wanted to see them light the torch. But he could not leave the old man alone in the snow. He slipped out of the gate just as it closed behind him.

But when he returned to where the old man had been, only Alexander's cloak lay in the snow. The old man was gone. Alexander picked up his cloak, then looked back at the gates. They were locked, only to be opened when the lighting was done. Already it was getting dark, and it was too late to go home. He sat down next to the gate to wait, wiping back his tears.

Then Alexander heard a creak and, to his surprise, the gate opened a crack. Alexander jumped to his feet and quickly ran inside. The town square was crowded with excited people. Alexander climbed up to a small window ledge where he could see.

Suddenly, from a building at the far side of the square, a large door opened and a man, dressed in a beautiful cloak lined with golden threads and precious jewels, walked from the building. A deep hush fell over the crowd. The Keeper of the Flame had arrived. In one hand he held a wreath, the symbol of Christmas. In the other was a small, flaming torch, with which the great torch would be lit.

"Let the offerings begin," said the Keeper.

The people of Noel lined up to give their gifts. As they laid their gifts beneath the tree, they loudly announced what they had brought.

"I am Julio, the minstrel," cried one. "My gift is a Christmas song, which will gladden the hearts of many." He played his song, then laid his pearwood lute beneath the tree.

"I am Marco, the writer," cried another. "I have written a great Christmas story, which will be shared for many years to come." And he laid a book bound in red and gold leather beneath the tree.

Then came the richest man in the city. "I am Maurizio, the jeweler. I have made a golden ornament for the tree."

The crowd clapped when they saw the ornament. It was of pure gold with red and green jewels, the colors of Christmas. Surely this was the best offering of the evening.

After all the people had laid down their gifts, the Keeper looked out into the crowd.

"Are there any more offerings?"

No one spoke. Alexander looked down, sad that he had nothing to give.

"Well, then, I shall choose the truest gift," the Keeper said. He looked at those who stood near the tree. "You have given much," he said, "but only one of you has given well."

Then the Keeper looked out to the crowd. "Come, Alexander."

Alexander looked around to see whom the Keeper spoke to. He had given no gift. Surely there was another named Alexander. But the Keeper looked right at him and smiled. "Come, my boy."

As Alexander neared the square, he recognized the Keeper. He was the old man in the snow. The Keeper put his hands on Alexander's shoulders and looked at the others. "You all passed by me tonight, lying in the snow outside the city gate. Only this boy stopped to help me. In your hurry to keep Christmas, you have forgotten Christmas.

"The truest gift of Christmas is the gift of self.
The flame of Christmas must first burn from within."
Then he handed the small torch to Alexander. "Light
our Christmas, dear boy. Light our Christmas."

Alexander touched the fire to the great, brass torch,
and it burst into a brilliant flame.

And it was said ever after that
never before had the flame burned
so bright or so true.